Goodnight, My Duckling

Goodnight,

My Duckling

NANCY TAFURI

SCHOLASTIC INC.
New York Toronto London Auckland Sydney
Mexico City New Delhi Hong Kong Buenos Aires

Sweet dreams to every little duckling—
and to *my* duckling, Cristina.

ISBN-13: 978-0-439-92412-2
ISBN-10: 0-439-92412-X

12 11 10 9 8 7 6 5 4 3 2 1   7 8 9 10 11 12/0

Printed in the U.S.A.   08

First Scholastic paperback printing, March 2007

Early one evening . . .

"Time for bed, my ducklings!"

"Goodnight,
little duckling."

"Sleep tight,
little duckling."

"See you in
the morning,
little duckling."

"Hurry home, little duckling."

"Are you lost, little duckling?"

"There you are, my duckling!"

"Sweet dreams,
little duckling."

"I love you, my duckling."

Goodnight.

Nancy Tafuri introduced Mama's venturesome little duckling in her Caldecott Honor-winner *Have You Seen My Duckling?* Ever since, she's wondered what else the loveable rascal has been up to. Now, twenty years and more than thirty children's books later, she's finally gotten the chance to find out.

Ms. Tafuri lives in Roxbury, Connecticut, with her husband and their daughter.